D1325094

Mary's Tiger

Story by **Rex Harley**

Pictures by *Sue Porter*

ORCHARD
BOOKS
LONDON

For two little tigers ·°· Anne~Valiha · Eve~Merina ·°·

(Mary's Tiger)

ORCHARD BOOKS
96 Leonard Street, London EC2A 4RH
Orchard Books Australia
14 Mars Road, Lane Cove, NSW 2066
First published in Great Britain 1990
First paperback publication 1991
Text copyright © Rex Harley 1990
Illustrations copyright © Sue Porter 1990
Designed by Sue Porter for Orchard Books
1 85213 160 8 (hardback)
1 85213 323 6 (paperback)
A CIP catalogue record for this book is available
from the British Library.
Printed in Belgium

Mary loved painting.

When Mrs Morris said, "Why don't you fill up the whole page with a nice colourful picture?", Mary started to draw her favourite animal: a bright, stripy tiger.

She drew its head first. It was bigger than she'd planned.

So when she came to draw the tiger's body, it had to be very small, with little legs and a tiny tail.

Because it looked a bit unhappy scrunched up like that, Mary painted a huge smile on the tiger's face.

She showed the picture to her mum.
"What a lovely tiger," her mum said.
"He looks very happy. Is he in love?"
Mary shook her head.

When Mary's dad saw the picture he said, "What's he smiling for, Mary? Has he just had a tasty meal?"

"No," Mary said.

"What a funny-looking tiger,"
said her big brother, Paul.
"Is he laughing at you?"

"No," said Mary. "You're all wrong."
But she wouldn't tell them why he was
smiling.

Mary's mother wanted to stick the painting on the kitchen wall with all Mary's other pictures.

But Mary wanted to put it in her bedroom.

She called the tiger Grin.
"Goodnight, Grin," she said at
bedtime. "Sleep well."

The room was very dark. Grin tried to sleep but he could not get comfortable.

He wriggled and twisted around. He got himself into some very awkward shapes.

And in the end he pushed so hard that,
before he knew what was happening,

he had fallen off the paper and landed
on the bed.

During the night Mary woke up. She was surprised to find a smiling tiger asleep on her pillow. He looked very comfortable.

Being careful not to wake him,
she reached up, took down the piece
of blank paper and threw it away.
   Then she climbed back into bed.

In the morning Mary's mum came to wake her. "Where's that lovely tiger of yours?" she asked.

"Don't worry," Mary said. "I've put him somewhere safe." And they went down to breakfast.